PIG the STINKER

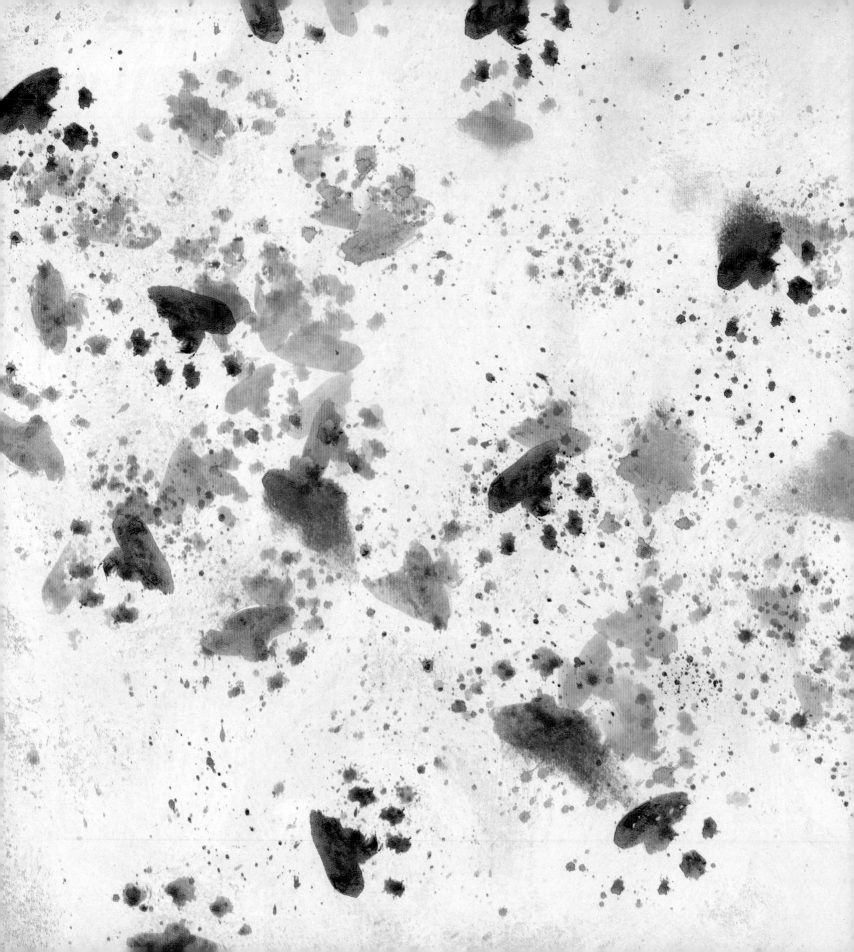

AWARD
for
NEATNESS

Trevor

For Mr. Murray,
who encouraged my nonsense.

ISBN 978-1-338-35371-6

10 9 8 7 6 5 4 3 2   19 20 21 22 23

Printed in the U.S.A.   169
This edition first printing 2019

The artwork in this book is acrylic (with pens and pencils) on watercolor paper.
The type was set in Adobe Caslon.

PIG the STINKER

Aaron Blabey

Scholastic Inc.

Pig was a pug
and I'm sorry to say,
his personal hygiene
was far from OK.

Pig liked to get dirty.
He frankly was RANK.

His paws could be frightful.

His fur often stank.

He wasn't offended
by odor or smell,

MILK
EXPIRED

and if you weren't careful,
he'd smell you as well.

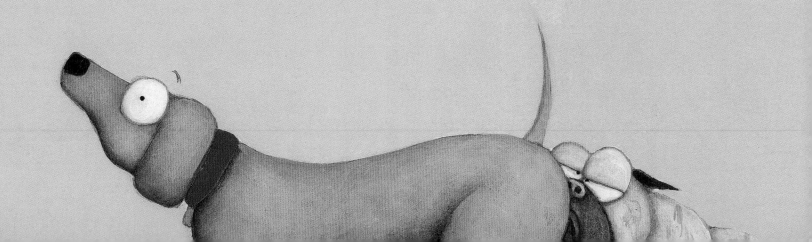

He'd play with all kinds of
unspeakable MUCK . . .

And do things to make you scream,

"DON'T
DO
THAT!
YUCK!"

He leaked out a stench
that could not be forgotten.
He reeked. He was rancid.
In short, he was rotten.

So BATH TIME was called!
"You stinky old mutt!
You need a good clean
from your ears to your butt!"

But Pig turned his tail.
And before you could grab it,

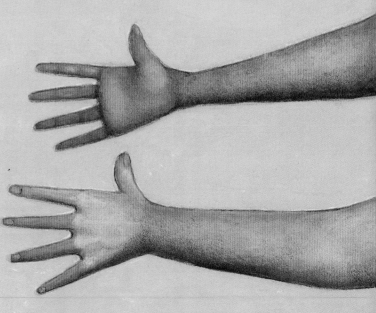

he was out of that room
like a foul little rabbit.

They chased him,
but Pig had a devious knack . . .

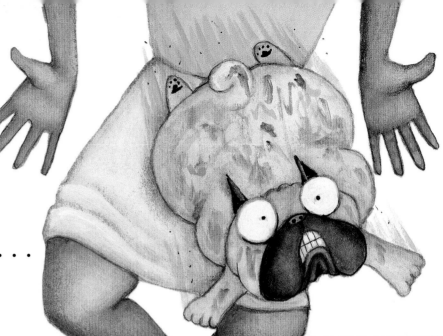

for ducking . . .

and weaving . . .

and doubling back.

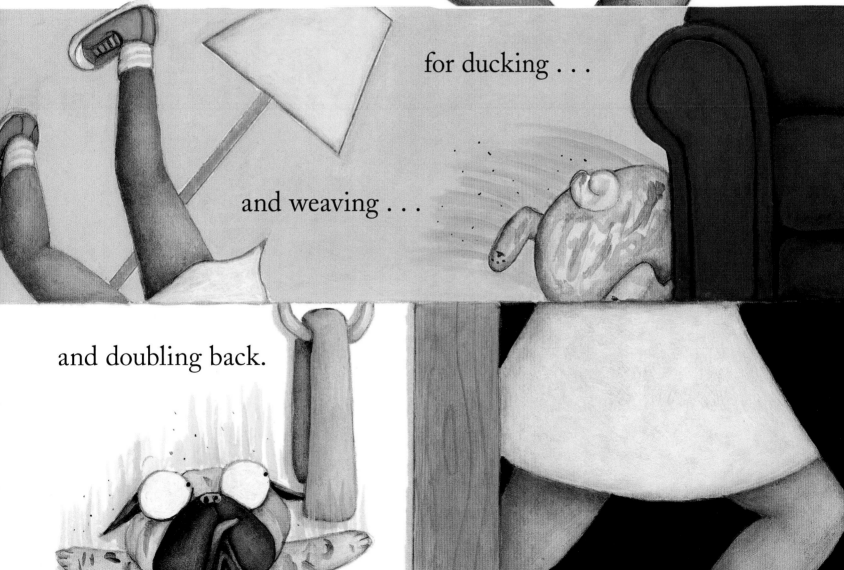

And once he had lost them,
he used a small toy . . .

to block up the pipes . . .

then he hooted with joy.

By the time they had found him,
Pig boogied with glee.

"YOU WON'T GET YOUR SOAPY OLD WATER ON ME!"

They watched as Pig gloated.

They watched as Pig crowed.

They

watched

as

Pig's

plan

made

the

bathroom...

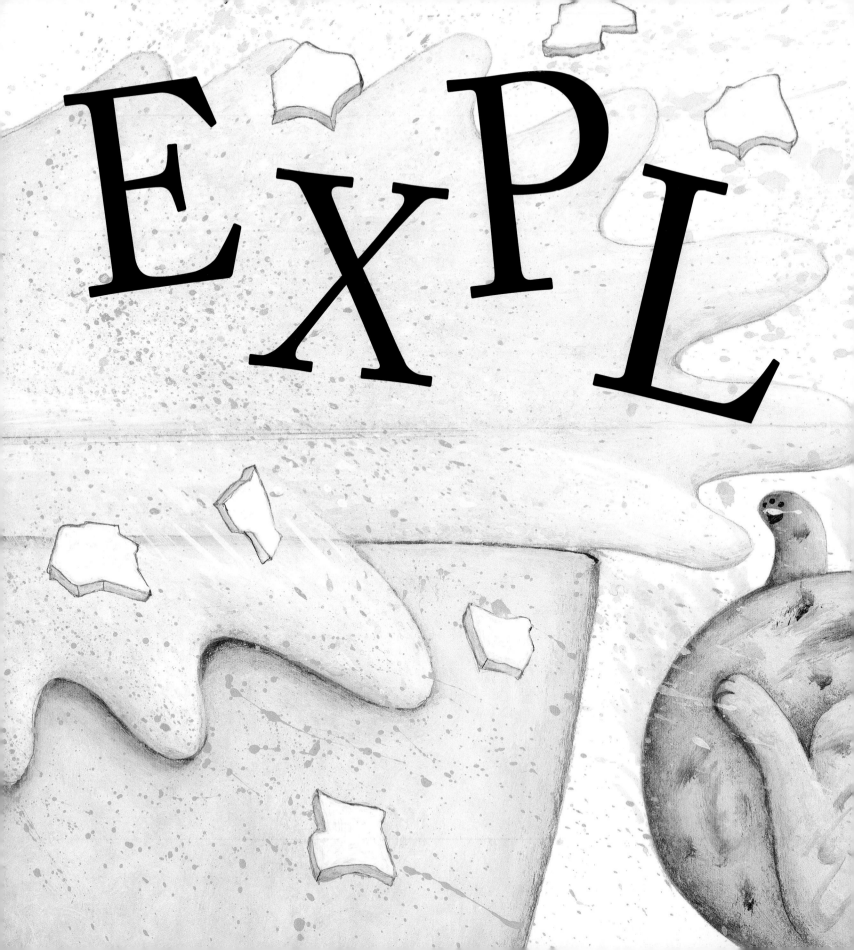

These days it's different,
I'm happy to say.
If you tell Pig it's bath time,
he won't disobey.

But although you can wash him
with soap, cloth, and towel,
there's no getting 'round it . . .

DOG-E-BATH

Pig is just foul.

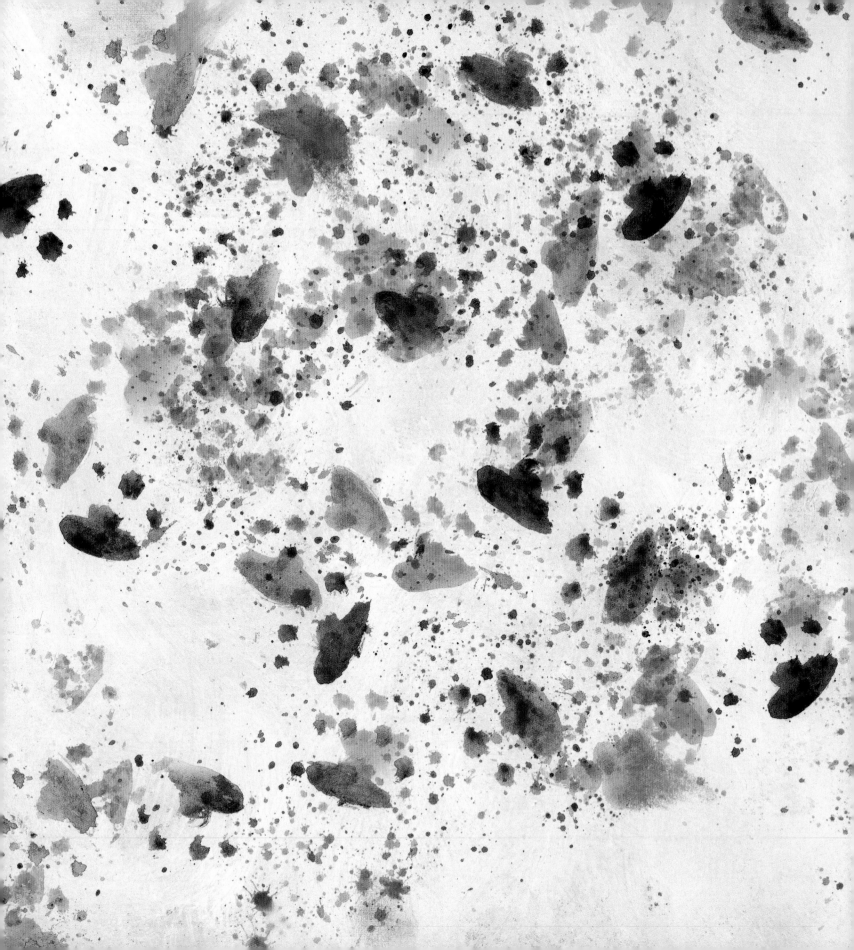

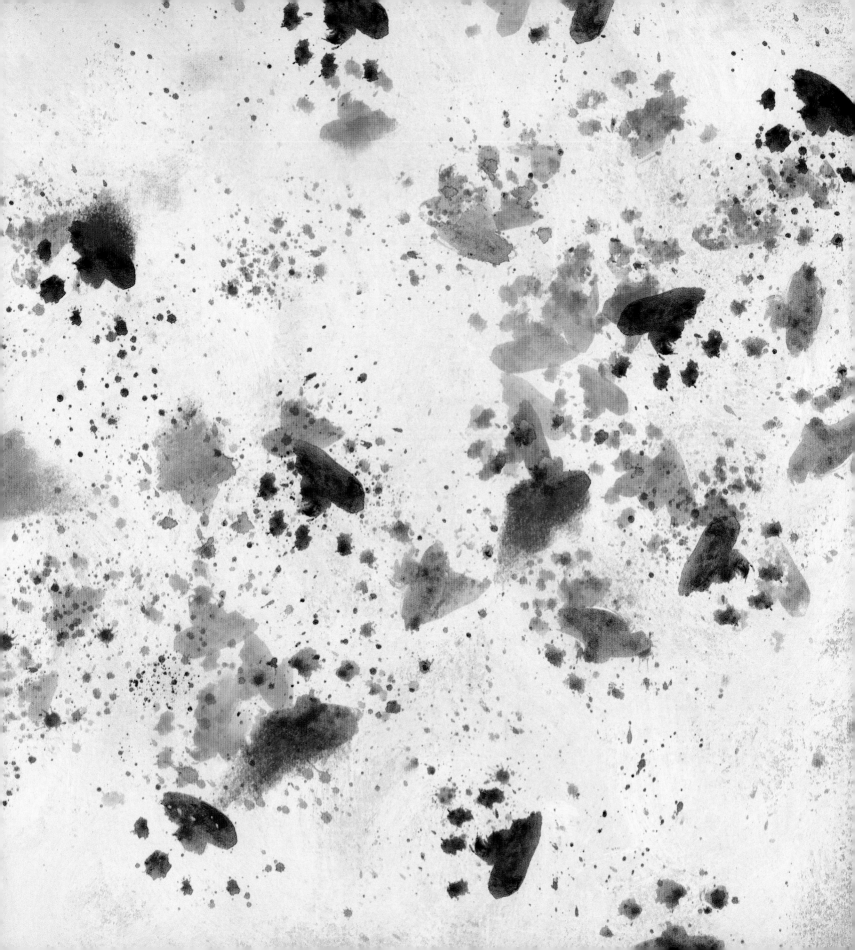